The Monster Diaries

Written by *Luciano Saracino* • Illustrated by P

meadowside
CHILDREN'S BOOKS

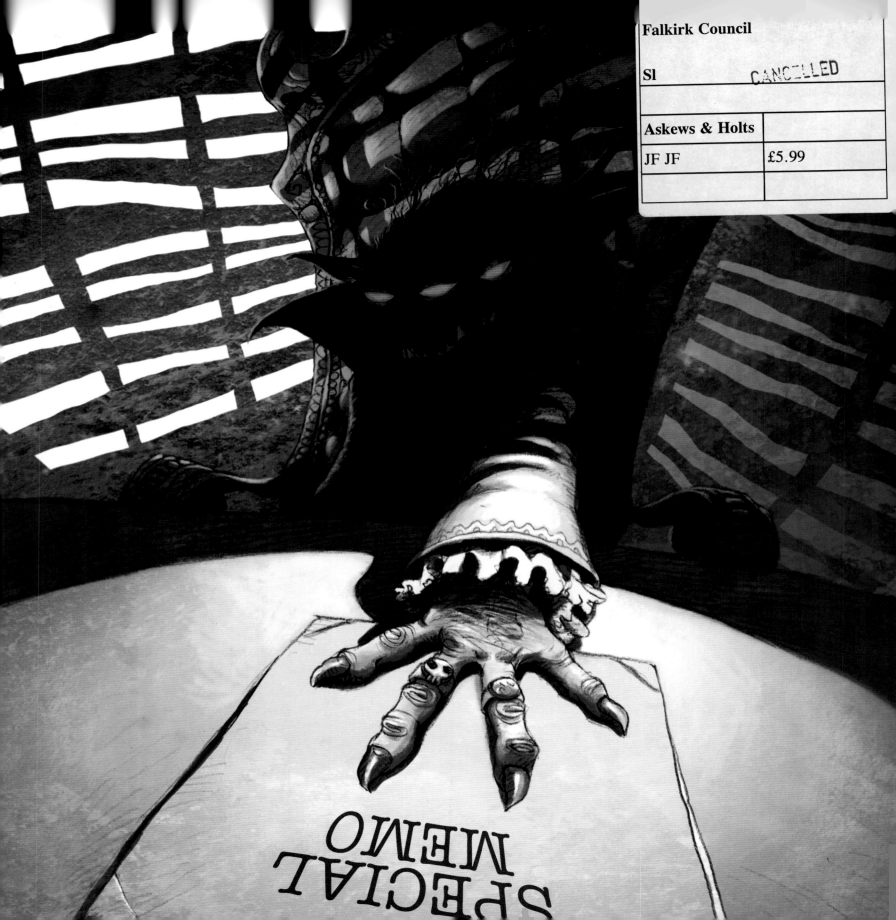

The Federation of Fright

It has come to our attention that human children have run out of nightmares. It appears children are no longer having bad dreams and this has led the Secret Committee for the Advancement of Real Evil (S.C.A.R.E) to conclude that not enough things are going bump in the night.

As part of our new 'Focus on Fear' campaign we have decided to throw a competition to find the Grisliest Ghoul. We will be studying the diary entries of each competitor in order to judge them on their terror tactics. The winner will be the proud owner of the famous Poisoned Chalice and will be presented with the Monster Medal.

Anyone wishing to enter should send a diary entry to the Federation of Fright by midnight on Monday.

Yours sincerely,

Z.Ombie

Zacharius Ombie (Head of Horror)

Monday 19   May

9   *Rust the chains.*

10   *Singing class. (Ask teacher to correct my 'boos!'*
      and 'oohs!' because people are laughing, instead
11   *of trembling with fear!)*

12   *Grave Owners Association meeting at Cemetery.*
      Agenda – discuss raising funds to buy glasses
13   *for Dracula who keeps going to bed in other*
      people's coffins.
14

15   *Buy more pretty sheets for the kids.*

16   *Remember to pick up clean sheets*
      from cleaners!

17

18   *The Ghost*

June

Wednesday

sunday monday tuesday WEDNESDAY thursday friday saturday

8:00	-chop onions
9:00	-Watch the soaps
10:00	-Read the newspaper
11:00	-Have a good cry
12:00	-chop more onions
13:00	-Watch the news
:00	-chop onions again
00	-Go out for cry

The cry Baby

1 2 3 4 5 6 7
8 9 10 11 12 13 14
15 16 17 18 19 20 21
24 25 26 27 28

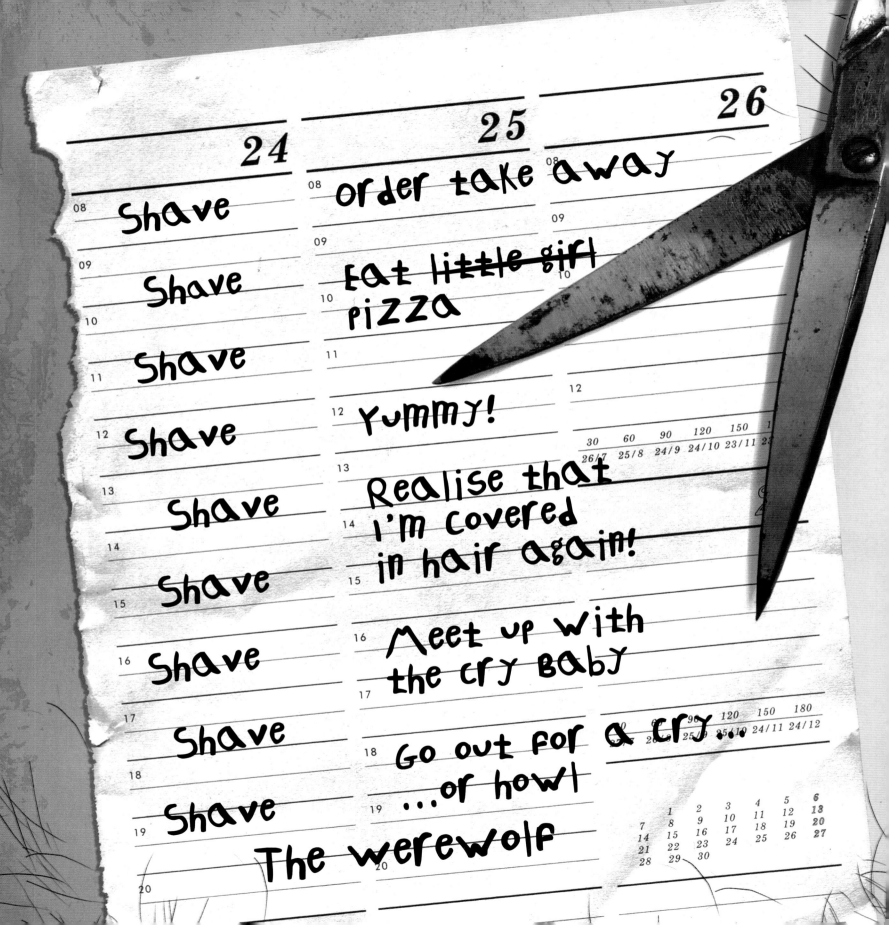

8:00 — Ski

— Prepare a glass of ice and ice (must not use too much ice because it gives me a headache)

9:00

— Go out hunting for a human and put him in the freezer

10:00 — Ski more (I really love it)

— Watch TV, freezing the image all the time

11:00 — Talk to other yetis coldly

12:00 — Air the igloo

— Look for the clever person who gave me a gas fire for my last birthday and tell him off (I bet it was Dracula - will send him some sun cream to see how he likes **13:00** bad jokes)

00 — Hibernate for a while

— See if I can borrow Werewolf's razor - I fancy a change of image

— Buy a coat (it might be cold without any fur)

The Abominable Snowman

1 2 3 4 5 6 7
8 9 10 11 12 13 14
16 17 18 19 20 21
24 25 26 27 28

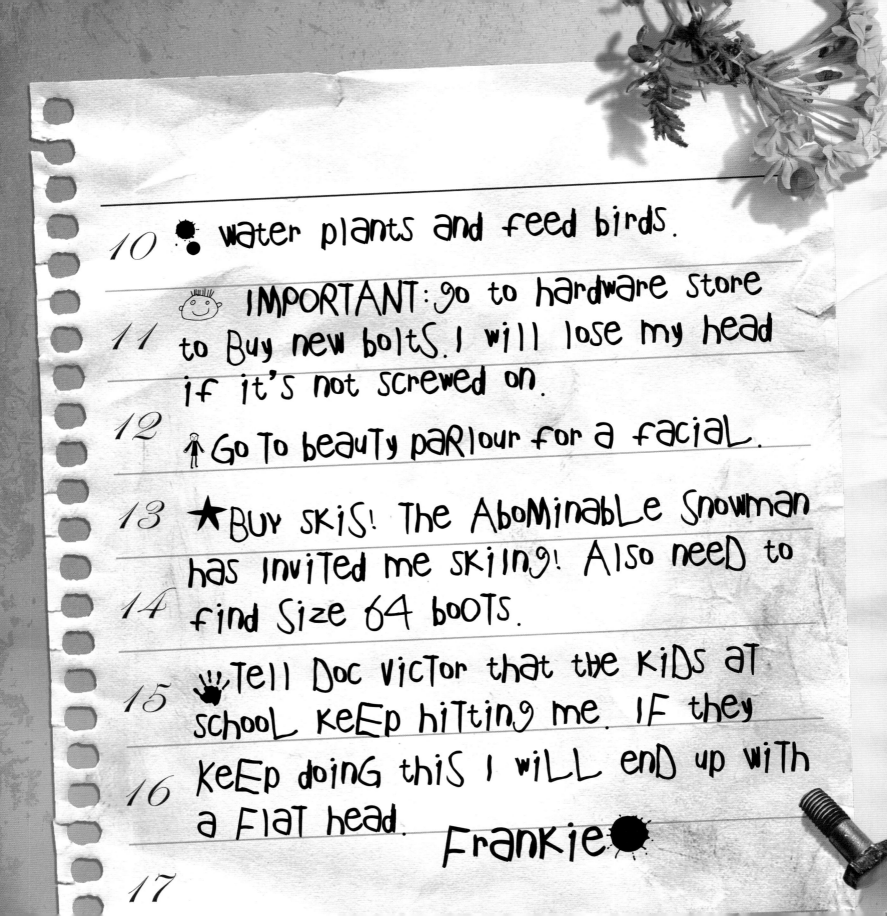

10 water plants and feed birds.

11 IMPORTANT: go to hardware store to Buy new bolts. I will lose my head if it's not screwed on.

12 Go To beauty parlour for a facial.

13 ★BUY SKIS! The Abominable Snowman has invited me skiing! Also need to

14 find Size 64 boots.

15 Tell Doc victor that the kids at school keep hitting me. If they

16 keep doing this I will end up with a Flat head. Frankie

17

20:00 Get alarm clock repaired – it keeps ringing early and I get up in daylight (there is nothing worse for a vampire's skin than sunlight and I can't face going to the beauty parlour and listening to Frankie complaining about the school kids again.)

21:00

22:00 Pick up cape at the cleaners – make sure they don't give me the Ghost's sheet again. (I'm in enough trouble with the Grave Owners Association.)

23:00

24:00 Moonbathe – I don't think this sun cream some clever person sent me will be any use...

1:00 Sharpen teeth – the years have worn them out.

2:00 Go out for a night on the tiles! Have a dance, drink some tomato juice, meet new people, watch a good horror film – but one with no vampires (I'm a bit scared of them).

3:00

4:00 Get back to the cemetery – make sure I lie down in the right coffin, the other grave owners are getting annoyed.

Dracula

5:00

1 2 3 4 5 6 7
8 9 10 11 12 13 14
15 16 17 18 19 20 21
22 23 24 25 26 27 28
29 30 31

Wednesday 2nd

January

Buy 500 metres of bandage at the pharmacy – these ones are getting a bit dusty.

Ask Frankie, Werewolf, the Crazy Scientist and the Ghost to help me change my bandages.

Talk about the old times (must remember NOT to invite Cry Baby – he is always crying and we can't hear each other over his din).

Get back to the museum – avoid the security guards!

Ring Daddy!

The Mummy

jueves
quinta
thursday

7

septiembre
setembro
september

8.00 — Wake up / **No, sleep for longer.**

8.30

9.00 — Go out for a jog / **I said sleep for longer!**

9.30 — **At the most, read the newspaper in bed.**

10.00

10.30 — Watch the news / **Watch cartoons.**

11.00

11.30 — Take a nap / **Ha! You should have slept in until later!**

12.00 — **Now, I feel like going out for a jog.**

12.30

13.00 — Go out with my girlfriend / **Go out with MY girlfriend.**

13.30

14.00 — Call the Crazy Scientist to separate me from this bore! /

14.30 — **Finally, we agree about something. But you're the bore.**

15.00

15.30 — Write a letter to the Grave Owners Association about

16.00 — the 'Two heads are better than one' graffiti at the

16.30 — graveyard / **How offensive! That certainly isn't true!**

17.00 — Sleep / **Oh yeah, right. You mean snore, more like!**

18.00

The Two-Headed **Man**

✗   Look for glasses

✗ Give Ghost a lesson in 'boos'
   – if I can manage it, surely he can!?

✓ Cancel appointment with the barber which
   some clever person pretending to be me
   made. Must have been the Snowman.
     Let's see how he feels when I give him
   a gas fire for his birthday!

✓ Ask Dracula whether he has seen my
   glasses (he keeps taking them by mistake)

✓   Speak to the Two-Headed Man. I'm sure I
   remember him saying he had one head too many...

✓ Ask the Crazy Scientist whether he used my
   glasses to invent anything. He always does
   the same thing and the only thing he does well
     is to do things wrong.

✗   Buy cream for bruises – walking around
   without seeing can be VERY painful

✓ Go to the doctor and ask why it is that I
   am always looking for my glasses.
     Is there something I'm not facing up to?

The Headless Man

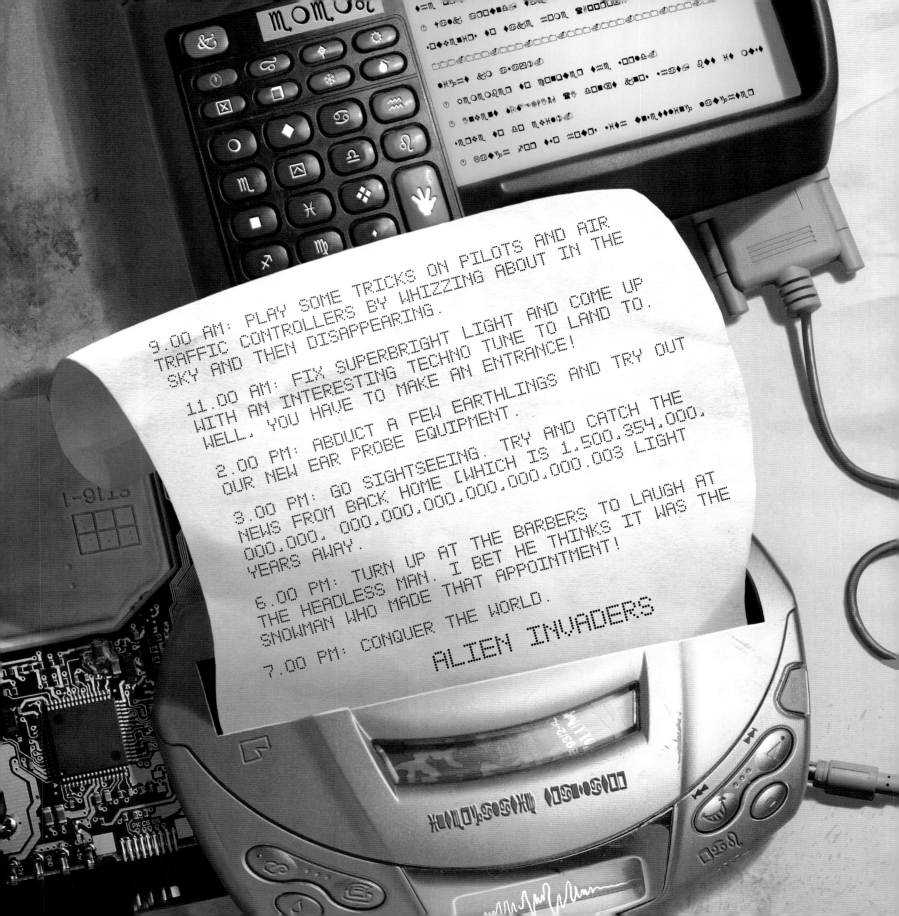

9.00 AM: PLAY SOME TRICKS ON PILOTS AND AIR TRAFFIC CONTROLLERS BY WHIZZING ABOUT IN THE SKY AND THEN DISAPPEARING.

11.00 AM: FIX SUPERBRIGHT LIGHT AND COME UP WITH AN INTERESTING TECHNO TUNE TO LAND TO. WELL, YOU HAVE TO MAKE AN ENTRANCE!

2.00 PM: ABDUCT A FEW EARTHLINGS AND TRY OUT OUR NEW EAR PROBE EQUIPMENT.

3.00 PM: GO SIGHTSEEING. TRY AND CATCH THE NEWS FROM BACK HOME (WHICH IS 1,500,354,000,000,000,000,000,000,000,000.003 LIGHT YEARS AWAY.

6.00 PM: TURN UP AT THE BARBERS TO LAUGH AT THE HEADLESS MAN. I BET HE THINKS IT WAS THE SNOWMAN WHO MADE THAT APPOINTMENT!

7.00 PM: CONQUER THE WORLD.

ALIEN INVADERS

10 Invent something evil to conquer world with!! Not sure what yet,
11 but make sure it's something REALLY EVil!!

12 Do evil laugh for 2 hours. BwaHaHaHahaha! Mwahahahahaha!

13 Drink honey tea to soothe throat. (Sore after 2 hours of evil laughing.)

14 Resit Quantum Physics Exam. Again. (This will be the 56th time!)

15 Conquer the World using this morning's invention (if I know what it is yet - make sure it's
16 EXTREMELY evil!!!!!) BwaHaHaha!

17 Failing all else, join the Alien Invaders and help them conquer world.

18 The Crazy Scientist

$$2 \times \sqrt{\dfrac{389 + 327}{25 \times 32 - 107}}$$

$$\sqrt{\dfrac{39^{35} \times 1}{8 \times 3 \times 3^4}}$$

$$2 + 2 = ?$$

$$\dfrac{\sqrt{442^3 \times 625}}{323 + 26} = \Omega = \dfrac{M + M + M^{\times 3}}{9039}$$

Friday

10:00 Confirm my attendance at the 27,856th annual Convention of Witches. This year's topic is "Wizards and Sorcerors. Why?".

11:00 Remind the Alien Invaders they MUST to respect Skyway Code.

Invite the girls to dinner.

12:00

13:00 Go to shops and buy leech tea, skimmed cockroach wings, seagull cavities, elephant forget-me-nots, swamp mud, deadly nighshade (I haven't seen mine since the Crazy Scientist came for coffee), varnished shadows, toilet paper, mobile phone top-up card and gas for the broomstick.

14:00

Turn self into a bear to carry all of this home.

6:00

17:00

19:00

Scrambled Frog

Ingredients (for 4 witches):
4 basilisk eggs
1 teaspoon of haunted swamp
1 teaspoon of stories which terrify at night
3 chopped cheeses
1 teaspoon of salt
8 kilos of butter

1. Wise woman of the forests, beat, but only slightly, the basilisk eggs and mix with the swamp, the stories which terrify at night, the salt and the chopped cheese.

2. Oh, Witch, you who scare everyone, put into the eight kilos of butter, generously covered with the eight kilos of butter.

3. You, who know so much, take it out and beat thoroughly. If it is not disgusting enough, put it back in for a bit. If, after all of this, the consistency is still not right, then, oh Witch of the night, who really, really, really should know a bit more than this... cook something else as you are obviously useless at this.

Ask the girls why this is called scrambled frogs – it doesn't even have frogs in it!

The Witch

Thank you for entering the
Grisliest Ghoul Competition.

And the winner is...

...none of you.
You're all useless!

For

Nacho "dreamer" Bernatene and to Miky "soul eyes" Saracino,
and to all children (and adults) who believe in monsters
and know how to laugh at them.

LS and PB

First published in 2005 by Meadowside Children's Books
185 Fleet Street, London EC4A 2HS
www.meadowsidebooks.com
This edition first published in 2011

Text © Luciano Saracino 2005 Illustrations © Poly Bernatene 2005

The rights of Luciano Saracino and Poly Bernatene to be identified
as the author and illustrator of this work have been asserted by them
in accordance with the Copyright, Designs and Patents Act, 1988

A CIP catalogue record for this book is available from the British Library

1 2 3 4 5 6 7 8 9 10

Paper used in the production of this book is a natural,
recyclable product from wood grown in sustainable forests